2013 may 23   Penworthy $10.00

Fun Dog, Sun Dog

story by
Deborah Heiligman

illustrations by
Tim Bowers

Marshall Cavendish Children

Marshall Cavendish, 99 White Plains Road, Tarrytown, NY, 10591
www.marshallcavendish.us/kids

Library of Congress Cataloging-in-Publication Data
Heiligman, Deborah.
Fun dog, sun dog / Deborah Heiligman ; illustrated by Tim Bowers.- 1st ed.
p. cm.
Summary: Although Tinka the dog can be described in many ways, she is always the right kind of canine for her owner.
ISBN: 978-0-7614-5162-4 (hardcover)   ISBN: 978-0-7614-5836-4 (paperback)   ISBN: 978-0-7614-5531-8 (board)
[1. Dogs–Fiction. 2. Pets–Fiction. 3. Stories in rhyme.] I. Bowers, Tim, ill. II. Title.
PZ8.3.H4132Fu 2005
[E]–dc22
2004023789

The illustrations are rendered in acrylic paint on gessoed three-ply bristol board.
Editor: Margery Cuyler
Printed in Malaysia (T)
1 2 3 4 5 6

Marshall Cavendish
Children

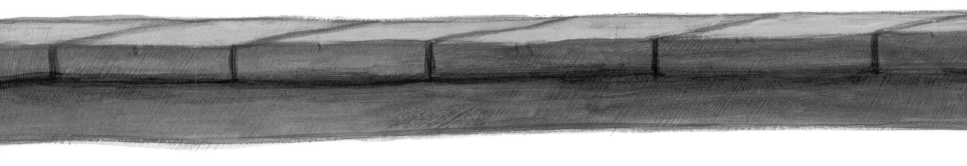

For Tinka, and for her friends Honeybee, Marigold, and Trippy -D.H.

To my friend, Jeff -T.B.

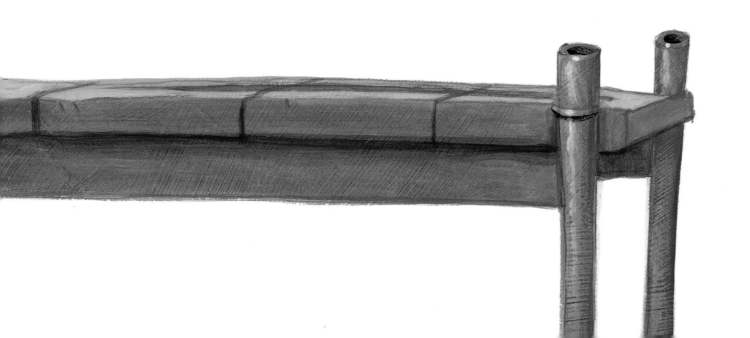

Tinka is a sweet dog,
a treat dog,
a jumping-up-to-greet dog.

A fun **dog**,
a sun **dog**,
a run-and-run-and-run dog.

A ride dog,
a slide dog,
a stay-right-by-my-side dog.

A beach dog,
a reach dog,
a something-new-to-teach dog.

Tinka is a dandy dog,
a sandy dog,
a snatching-all-my-candy dog.

A howl dog,
a yowl dog,
a crawl-beneath-my-towel dog.

An ocean dog,
a motion dog,
a grabbing-suntan-lotion dog.

A sticky dog,
an icky dog,
an icky-sticky-licky dog.

Tinka is a hot dog,
a trot dog,
a runs-away-a-lot dog.

A fair dog,
a bear dog,
an I-don't-want-to-share dog.

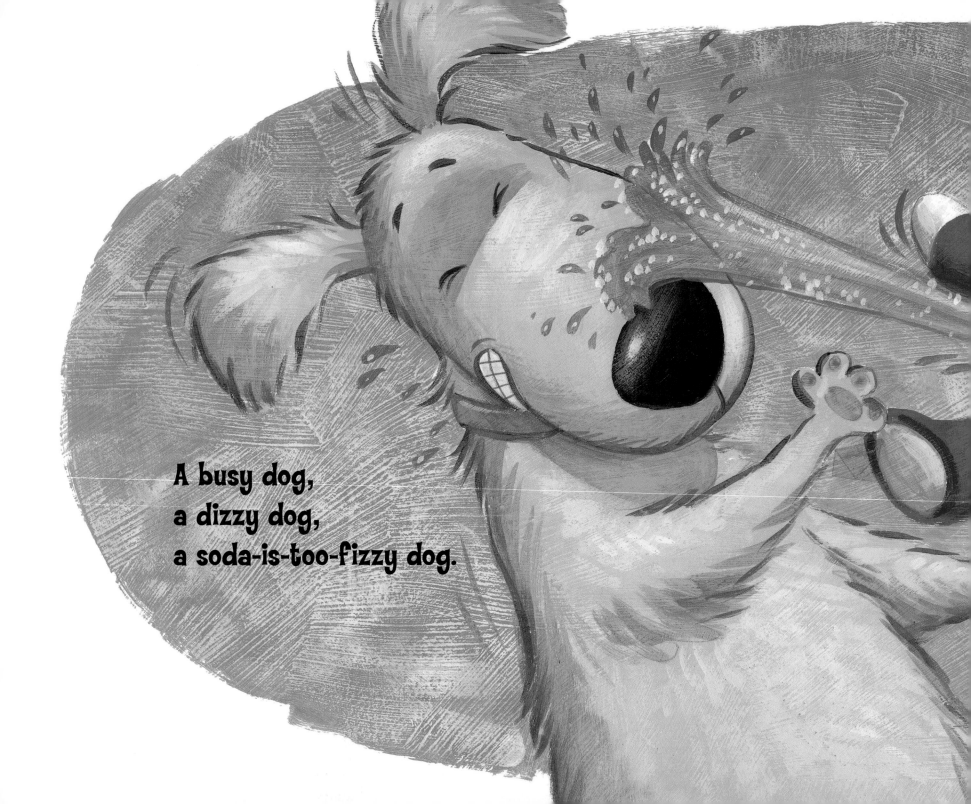

A busy dog,
a dizzy dog,
a soda-is-too-fizzy dog.

Tinka is a park dog,
a bark dog,
a take-me-home-it's-dark dog.

A night dog,
a fright dog,
a something's-not-quite-right dog.

A *Hey!* dog,
a sprayed dog,
a skunk-got-in-the-way dog.

Tinka is a stink dog,
a blink dog,
a too-big-for-the-sink dog.

A tub dog,
a rub dog,
a scrub-a-dub-a-dub dog.

Tinka is a prancy dog,
a dancy dog,
a brushed-and-combed-and-fancy dog.

A nap dog,
a wrap dog,
a climb-up-in-my-lap dog.

A care dog,
a share dog,
a when-I-need-her-there dog.